A Note to Parents

Read to your child...

★ Reading aloud is one of the best ways to develop your child's love of reading. Read together at least 20 minutes each day.

★ Laughter is contagious! Read with feeling. Show your child that reading is fun.

★ Take time to answer questions your child may have about the story. Linger over pages that interest your child.

...and your child will read to you.

★ Do not correct every word your child misreads. Instead, say, "Does that make sense? Let's try it again."

★ Praise your child as he progresses. Your encouraging words will build his confidence.

You can help your Level 2 reader.

★ Keep the reading experience interactive. Read part of a sentence, then ask your child to add the missing word.

★ Read the first part of a story. Then ask, "What's going to happen next?"

★ Give clues to new words. Say, "This word begins with *b* and ends in *ake*, like *rake, take, lake.*"

★ Ask your child to retell the story using her own words.

★ Use the five *W*s: WHO is the story about? WHAT happens? WHERE and WHEN does the story take place? WHY does it turn out the way it does?

Most of all, enjoy your reading time together!

—**Bernice Cullinan, Ph.D.,**
Professor of Reading, New York University

Published by Reader's Digest Children's Books
Reader's Digest Road, Pleasantville, NY U.S.A. 10570-7000 and
Reader's Digest Children's Publishing Limited,
The Ice House, 124-126 Walcot Street, Bath UK BA1 5BG
Copyright © 1999 Reader's Digest Children's Publishing, Inc.
All rights reserved. Reader's Digest Children's Books is a trademark and
Reader's Digest and All-Star Readers are registered trademarks of
The Reader's Digest Association, Inc. Fisher-Price trademarks are used
under license from Fisher-Price, Inc., a subsidiary of
Mattel, Inc., East Aurora, NY 14052 U.S.A.
©2000 Mattel, Inc. All Rights Reserved.
Printed in Hong Kong.
10 9 8 7 6 5

Library of Congress Cataloging-in-Publication Data

Hood, Susan.
    My tooth is loose! / by Susan Hood ; illustrated by Julie Durrell.
       p. cm. — (All-star readers. Level 2)
    Summary: Ben is anxiously waiting for his loose tooth to fall out so he
    can be like the other kids in his class.
    ISBN 1-57584-310-2
    [1. Teeth—Fiction. 2. Stories in rhyme.]
    I. Durrell, Julie, ill. II. Title. III. Series.
    PZ8.3.H7577My   1999   [E]—dc21   99-19687

My Tooth Is Loose!

by Susan Hood
illustrated by Julie Durrell

2
All-Star Readers®
Reader's Digest Children's Books™
Pleasantville, New York • Montréal, Québec

My tooth is loose.
It won't come out.
My tooth is all I think about.

I wiggle it when I first get up.

I wiggle it when I pat my pup.

I wiggle it when I do my math.

I wiggle it when I take a bath.

My best friend Paul just lost a tooth.

Leanne lost three,

and so did Ruth.

Paul put a tooth up on the wall.

I wish that
I could be like Paul.

I'll pull my tooth out with a string.

See what happens? Not a thing.

I'll munch an apple,

bite a pear.

See what happens?

It's still there!

Mom says, "Relax.
Don't worry, Ben.
It WILL come out."

I wonder when.

I wake up suddenly in the night.
My tooth is gone—
it's nowhere in sight!

I lost my tooth! Oh, no! OH, NO!
I lost my tooth! Where did it go?

It must be somewhere
in my bed.
Look! There it is,
beneath my spread!

I held it close to me all night.
I dreamed I saw a tiny light.

A fairy flew in while I slept.
She was a dream, I think.
Except…

When I woke up and rubbed my eyes,

I found a treat, to my surprise!
Now I am rich and best of all—

I have a smile like my friend Paul!

Words are fun!

Here are some simple activities you can do with a pencil, crayons, and a sheet of paper. You'll find the answers at the bottom of the page.

———— ★ ————

1. Which word means the same as the word on the left?

wiggle (walk, eat, jiggle)

pat (tap, skip, roar)

string (tree, cord, cake)

relax (bounce, fall, rest)

lost (dark, missing, old)

munch (chew, spit, yawn)

pull (drink, tug, kick)

2. Big words often have little words inside them. Cover some of the letters of each word with your fingers to see what little words you can find.

wiggle	**happens**
string	**somewhere**
suddenly	**nowhere**

3. Match the words that rhyme — even though they may not be spelled the same way.

up	**math**
bath	**wall**
string	**Ruth**
Paul	**pup**
tooth	**thing**

4. Find two words in the story that rhyme with:

head	**ring**
path	**low**
hen	

5. Rearrange the words below to make a sentence.

my	**night**	**I**	**tooth**
at	**lost**		